Author biography

ABOUT THE AUTHOR IN BRIEF

Born of a middle class family, the author, Md. Anowar Islam is a lawyer and journalist by profession and passed his Matriculate examination from S. Ali Govt. Aided High School, Sukchar (Assam) in 1977 and completed his Arts Graduation from Tura Govt. College (Meghalaya) in 1981. He pursued his higher studies in law in J.B. Law College, Guwahati and obtained LL.B degree from there subsequently and completed Master Degree in Arts from Gauhati University thereafter in 1990. He also passed the NCTVT training course in stenography from Tura ITI, Tura earlier. He entered government service early in 1981 and served various departments both under State mad Central Governments at Guwahati, Goalpara and Tura. He also served as Lecturer in Goalpara Law College for sometime, as also in Kazi & Zaman College, New Bhaitbari and then in Hatsingimari College. He joined the Tura Bar Association sometime in 1992. His journalistic works started practically as back as in 1979 immediately after successfully participating in the Competition Success Review Essay Contest

No.293 and has by now composed a large number of poems in English, Assamese, Bengalee and Hindi as well. He has also established a good rapport as an outstanding educationist, author, writer of note books and poet and has had a lot of published works done and contributed to different dailies of the North Eastern Region and joined as an active mofussil newspaper reporter sometime in 1991 and associated himself with The Assam Tribune, The North-East Times, The Meghalaya Guardian, The Shillong Times and as a freelancer to The Telegraphs etc. and so on so forth. His poetic compositions have come to be published in different local books and magazines while his efforts to publish a local BI-lingual weekly, Sapta-Dhwani from Hatsingimari (Assam) from February, 2000 as the founder editor, although could not be successfully carried through, yet brought him acclamation from all corners. He has associated with different social organizations and served as Members and Advisers in different organizations like the Meghalaya Board of Wakfs, Assam Unnati Sabha, Animal Welfare Board of India, Total Literacy Campaign, West Garo Hills district, Meghalaya, Founder President of Hatsingimari Press Club and so on. He has also been honoured with Rashtriya Rattan Award in 2004 , followed by an Award given away by a Dhubri-based local weekly publications group. He has been a great social activist rendering social services all through his life in association with Red-Cross Society and many other local NGOs and will continue to serve the people as such in all future to come. At present he is practicing as an Advocate under Hatsingimari Bar Association, and holding a key position of Headman in his

HISTORY, GROWTH & DEVELOPMENT OF NEWSPAPERS IN LOWER ASSAM

Newspapers In Lower Assam

MD. ANOWAR ISLAM

HISTORY, GROWTH & DEVELOPMENT OF NEWSPAPERS IN LOWER ASSAM

ISBN 978-93-5458-051-2

Published in India 2021 by Pencil

A brand of
One Point Six Technologies Pvt. Ltd.
123, Building J2, Shram Seva Premises,
Wadala Truck Terminal, Wadala (E)
Mumbai 400037, Maharashtra, INDIA
E connect@thepencilapp.com
W www.thepencilapp.com

own eleca with sufficient pull over the mass people.

-------Author.

CONTENTS

Chapter-1

History, Growth & Development Of Newspapers/Journalism In Lower Assam
(Total Journalist in Assam : 2000 appx. as in 1998)

It is indeed a very difficult task to trace the exact chronological history, growth and development of news papers, news reporting and journalism in any particular State of a country, far less to speak about a belt like that of Lower Assam Division in the North East India. And yet an effort is nevertheless being sought to be made hereunder towards tracing the history, growth and development of news papers, news reporting and journalism in Lower Assam down Kamrup district of the State through this small piece of work of mine under mounting pressures put up on me by some of the young, energetic and upcoming news-reporters and media persons of our place here at Hatsingimari , of Assam in the form of an article.

The materials available in hand are not adequate enough to trace the correct history, growth and development of news papers, news reporting and journalisim in Lower Assam Division of the North East with exact locational descriptions where exactly from one or other particular newspapers or magazines came to be founded and published. Yet whatever little effort is made here to present the article with limited materials in hand, it is highly expected to add much more to the glamour of the "Smriti Grantha" called "AAMAR KHOBOR" sought to be published and released by the organizers on the auspicious occasion of the Opening Ceremony of "Mahkuma Press Council,Hatsingimari' shortly after.

I am, however, inclined to draw a little reference from different sources including the Profiles of Journalists of Assam published under the aegis of the Committee for Celebration of 150 Years of News Papers in Assam in 1998 and select as many as 6(six) different districts, namely, Barpeta, Bongaigaon, Goalpara, Kokrajhar, Dhubri including Nalbari districts to be the major constituent districts of Lower Assam Division and begin to pen down the history, growth and development of news papers, news reporting and journalism in Lower Assam Division ditrictwise.

It may not be out of place however not note here that Nalbari district, which was earlier constituted as a part of erstwhile Kamrup district, is being given a slight coverage here under Lower Assam Division only on the basis of my personal assessment and consideration as a matter of geographical proximity and structural marriage of convenience and not repeat not in conformity with whether it is so considered at the administrative level under the Government of Assam or not. The districtwise history about the growth and development of newspapers, news reportings and journalism in this Division is discussed as under:-

BARPETA DISTRICT

The growth and development of news media in Barpeta district appears to have begun and reached a height surpassing a total of more than 159 journalists excluding the new generation coming up from different remote and rural areas of the district and rendered services to different newspapers that grew up and developed in the course of time, more precisely during the post-Independence period, with a rare trace of one or two found to have grown up and developed here or there before Independence, a little data of some of the noted journalists have been collected and along with their works and endeavours towards the growth and development of newspapers and newspapers reporting including journalism in the district including the State of Assam and elsewhere are furnished hereinafter below:-

The post-Independence growth of journalism in Barpeta district witnessed a host of pre-Independence period intellectuals as well engaging themselves in the epoch-making task, which ultimately led to a decadewise gradual development of newspapers, newsreporting and journalism followed by registration of an increasingly higher number of newer and youthful intellectuals joining hand and working for achieving all social goals and public development, and some of the prominent born intellectuals contirubuting their mites towards fulfilling the noble mission a caused a numerous daily newspapers, magazines, weeklies, fortnightlies come up to be published in different capacities within and outside the district as are enumerated hereunder

The beginning decades of pre-Independence period upto the forties startaing from 1918, witnessed the growth of journalists and newspapers etc. in Barpeta district starting with Dharma Kingkor Goswami, born at Piplagaon, Pathsala of Barpeta district, started working as

Barpeta Correspondent, Asomiya in 1918, Desk Assistant, Chetna edited by Ambikagiri Roy Choudhury. Debendra Nath Sharma, born at Karakuchi in 1904, Editor, Asom Raiz in 1967-83, Santidoot in 1953, Congress in 1950, Raiz in 1934, Milon in 1929, received Freedom Fighter's Tamrapatara. Dr. Dinanath Sharma, born at Bamunkuchi, Pathsala, worked as Editor, Awahon (Monthly News Magazine) in 1929, Editor, Porijat Aru Pokhila (Child Magazine). Sotish Ch. Sharma, born at Borbila in 1913, worked as local correspondent, Asom Batori in 1951-67, Hindustan Standard in 1932-33. Horgobinda Sharma, born at Bamunkuchi, Pathsala, worked as Asstt, Editor, Awahon (Monthly News Magazine), Editor, Porijat Aru Pokhila (Child Magazine) in 1935-39, as Kolkata-based Reporter in Assam Newspapers. Sonapoti Deb Sharma, born at Muguria, Pathsala, worked as Publisher/Editor, Sevak in 1935. Hori Prashad Brahmachari, born at Barpeta, died in 1943, Editor/Publisher, Satya Barta before Independence. Bishnu Kingkor Goswami, born in 1925 at Pipla, started working as Asst Editor, Notun Asomiya, Sadhin Asom (1947). Gokul Pathak, born in 1927 at Bornagar worked as Publisher/Editor, Amar Desh (Saptahik from 1968 for some years), Rupantar (1947-67). Prodip Kr Das, born at Barpeta Goliyahati started working as Barpeta Correspnodent, Notun Asomiya in 1948-54, Transport Chronicle (Bombay). Dhorinidhar Das, born at Bhutepuwabari, Pathsala worked as Publisher and Editor, Abhijan in 1948. Bhubeneswar Barman, born in 1923 at Kalojeerapara, Patacharkuchi Correspondent, Notun Asomiya 1948-67. Ataul Ch Saikia, born at Daishingori on August 13, 1922, noted Trade Union leader, Sub-Editor, Notun Asomiya in 1948-49. Paramananda Goswami, born at Pathacharkuchi, Barpeta,worked as Correspondent,Notun Asomiya, Asomiya,Saptahik Jonombhumi from 1950-70.

During the beginning of the fifties Ambikacharan Pathak, born in 1920, died in 1986 at Barpeta, worked as local correspondent, Notun Asomiya for about 5 years. Domborudhar Das, born in 1925, died in 1991 at Barpeta, worked as local correspondent, Notun Asomiya, Ananda Bazar Patrika in 1951, Representative, Saptahik Jonombhumi, Frontier Times, Editor, Nobodhara Kamrupa, Deepshikha, Joint Editor, All Assam Small Newspapers Convention. Troloikya Dutta, born in 1930 at Ratanpur, started working as Commercial Artist, The Assam Tribune, later as Cartoonist in 1966, Artist, Notun Asomiya in 1952-57, 1963, Editor, Sristi in 1978-91, Charu Aru Karu Kolar Pramanpatra. Prabhat Ch Khatoniyar, born in 1932 at Kaljiropara, worked as Sub-Editor, Shantidoot in 1956, Sub-Editor, then Asst Editor, Dainik Asom in 1965-95, served as President of Working Journalist Association in 1986, General Secretary, North East Journalist Forum in 1987. Ramesh Ch Saha, born at Tarabarigaon, presently living at Barpeta Road, started working as correspondent, Jugantar in 1956-71. Kamal Ch Bayon, born in1935 at Jonia Shatra, worked as local correspondent, Ajir Asom, Hindi Sentinel, Notun Asomiya, 1960-68, Dharmayug, Biswamitra, Briish 1958-75.

During the sixties, Hiten Nath Bhattacharyya, born in 1939 at Gomura, Sorthebari, started working as Sub-Editor, Dainik Asom in 1965-68, Asst Editor, Saptahik Nobodhara in 1963-64, Translator, Notun Asomiya in 1961-62, Asst Editor, Yubak in 1964-65. Girija Prasad

Das, born in 1934 at Barpeta, started working as Guwahati Correspondent, Saptahik Jonombhumi in 1962, Sub-Editor, Frontier Times in 1963, Shillong Representative, Asom Batori, worked in UNI, Shillong office in 1965, President, Reporters' Guild. Satish Ch Choudhury, born in 1942 at Pathsala, started working as local correspondent, Dainik Asom in 1965, Dainik Janambhumi in 1971, Ajir Asom in 1987, Sentinel,Hindi, The Sentinel, Saptahik Janambhumi in 1962-71, Chief Editor, Alipona (Tri-monthly) in 1970, Principal Secretary, Asom Sahitya Sabha in 1989-91, 1994-95. The name of Ambikagiri Roy Choudhury, born in 1885 at Barpeta, died in 1967, Founder and Editor, Assam Bandhob, published Chetona, who received Sahitya Academy Award, is best remembered for his outstanding services during this period. Achyut Lahkar, born at Pathsala, Editor, Deepawali in 1962. Mukunda Sharma, born at Patacharkuchi on June 1, 1934, worked under Sadiniya Nobo Yug in 1964-66, Janambhumi in 1968-71, Saptahik Nilachal in 1975-77. Hrishikesh Boruah, born in 1930 at Barpeta worked under Indian News and Feature Agency (INFA), Sub-Editor, The Frontier Times (1965-67). Ilimuddin Dewan, born in 1937 at Chenimari, started working as Publisher/Editor, Ajan in 1965-90.

Likewise, during the seventies, Dhonbindu Sharma, worked as Joint Editor, Bwakha (Magazine) in 1972. Heramba Sharma, worked as Joint Editor, Bwakha (Magazine) in 1972. Sunil Kr Das, born in 1945 at Barpeta, started working as local correspondent, Agradoot in 1976, Purbachal in 1989-92, Asom Songbad in 1991, Mahajati in 1981-83, Rashtriya Batori in 1979-91, Notun Asomiya in 1975, Prantabashi in 1976-78, Amar Desh in 1973. Koruna

Dutta, born in 1954 at Barpeta, started working as local correspondent, Pratidin in 1986, Batori in 1982, Mohajati in 1979-82, Prantabashi in 1975, Editor, Simanta in 1980. Mukut Adhikary, born in 1959 at Sorbhog, started working as a local correspondent, Mahajati in 1976. Sukumar Bosumatary, born in 1948, died in 1996 at Lecheragaon, Kordoiguri, worked as Editor, Argeng, 1977-78, Joint Editor, The Bodo, 1984, Asst, Editor, 17th Bodo Sahitya Sabha Conference, 1976. Nageswar Das, born in 1955 at Batiyamari, started working as local Correspondent, Agradoot in 1979, Suchana in 1994, Borpeeth, Gana Batori, Sonkiyoni, Amar Desh. Kumar Meen Das, born in, 1956 at Metuakuchi, Barpeta, started working as local correspondent, Agradoot in 1980, Ajir Asom in 1988-90, Rashtriya Batori in 1984, Co-Editor, Ami in 1991-92.

During the eighties, Anjan Sharma, born at Pathsala in 1960, worked as Editor, Saptahik Nilachal in 1989-94, Mohabahu in 1980. Sokina Khatun, born at Barpeta, worked in Desk, Jagoron in 1980-82. Silpir Prithvi. Katindra Souragiriyari, born at Siyarguri, Salbari in 1964, started working as correspondent in Bodo Saptahik Thulonga, Editor, Sanshree in 1981, Rajalema in 1986, Bibungthi in 1989, Bishombi in 1986, Bihoushali in 1994, received Someshwari Sahitya Award 1995 given away in Goreswar Conference of Bodo Sahitya Sabha. Chakreshwar Deka, born in 1961 at Sorthebari, started working as local correspondent, Dainik Asom in 1993, Editor, Publisher, Jironi in 1983, Editor, Raizmel in 1983. Munin Bayon, born in 1961 at Barpeta, worked as Asst, Editor, Dainik Agradoot 1995, Sub-Editor to Chief Sub-Editor, Notun Dainik 1988-93, Co-Editor, Ajir Somoy, 1985-87. Somnath Talukdar, born in 1962 at Bohori started working as local Correspondent, Asomiya Pratidin in 1995, Borpeeth in 1987-89. Dwijendra Nath Das, born in 1961 at Barpeta, started working as Sports Correspondent, Ajir Batori in 1994,Khel Songbad in 1990, Staff Reporter, Borpeeth in 1987-90. Sadhiram Kalita, born in 1939 at Konimara, worked as Tihu Correspondent, Dainik Asom in 1988-93, Saptah Darpan in 1992, Saptahik Nilachal in 1993-94, Deubar in 1992, Amorjyoti in 1991-92, Mahanagar in 1990-91, Saptahik Asom in 1989-91, Representative, Nobotorang in 1991, Shashot in 1991. Lohit Ch Deka, born in 1914, died in 1992, at Sorthebari started working as local correspondent, Notun Asomiya, Dainik Asom, Batori, Santidoot, Jonombhumi, Asom Raiz, Nilachal, Sohojatri, Yugadharma, Advisor, Sorthebari Anchalik Journalist Association in 1988. G L Agarwala, born in 1940 at Barpeta Road, started his career as Founder and Managing Director of G L Publications Ltd (Guwahati) and G L Media Services Ltd (Jorhat) and as Editor, Purbanchal Prahari (Hindi Daily) on May 16, 1989, The Meghalaya Guardian (English Daily) on January 1, 1990, Managing Editor, North East Times on October 2, 1990 and Puwali (Assamese Fortnightly) on November 1, 1991. Abdul Jalil, born at Barpeta in 1969, sarted working as Sub-Editor, Saptahik Mujaheed in 1990. Hiranya Kumar Nath, born in 1954 at Gobordhan, started working as Bilashipara Correspondent, Ajir Batori in 1991, Notun Dainik in 1990, Ajir Asom in 1990, Rongpur in 1994. Koruna Mohan Sharma, born at Baghmara in 1958, worked in AIR, local correspondent, Purbachal in 1991, The North East Times in 1990, The North East Observer in 1992, The News Front in 1992, Amorjyoti in 1992, Agrogoti in 1992.

The nineties witnessed a host of journalists and newspapers like : Abdur Rahman, born in 1966 at Roumary, worked as Editor, Saptahik Mujaheed in 1991, Executive Editor, Noor. Poresh Deb Choudhury, born in 1967 at Pathsala started working as Sub-Editor, later Staff Reporter, Ajir Asom in 1993-95, Editor, Saptah Darpan in 1992, Gyan Vigyan Barta in 1992-93, Editing Assistant, Vigyan Jeuti in 1991-93. Dhiman Talukdar, born in 1968 at Sorbhog, started working as Cultural Representative, Asom Ganamot in 1991, Asstt, Editor, Gyan Vigyan in 1991-93. Abdul Khalek, born at Bortari, Baghbor, Barpeta, started working as Editor, Saptahik Sombar in 1991, Asst, Editor, Kongkon in 1993-94, Editor, Banas in 1994, as Guwahati Representative, Kolkata Weekly Column in 1995. Priya Mohan Kakati, born in 1939 at Bohori Shatra, started working as Guwahati Correspondent, Hajor Batori in 1992. Ranjan Lal Sharma, born at Barpeta in 1973, worked as local correspondent, Ajir Songbad in 1994, Saptahik Deubar in 1992, Representative, Suchana in 1994, Third Best Prize Winner of Ajir Songbad in 1994. Somoy Prabah in 1991. Ratan Soud, born at Barpeta in 1965, started working as Executive Editor, Budhbar in 1995, Staff Reporter/Sub-Editor, Notun Dainik in 1992-95, Sub-Editor, The North East Times for sometime. Brojogopal Das, born in 1953 at Barpeta, started working as Sports Correspondent, Dainik Asom in 1993.. Sukur Ali, born in 1948 at Chenimari, started working as Proof Reader, Weekly Mujaheed in 1994. Nobjeet Das, born in 1968 at Barpeta, started working as local correspondent, Asomiya Pratidin in 1995, Kishloi in 1994.

BONGAIGAON DISTRICT

HISTORY, GROWTH & DEVELOPMENT OF NEWSPAPERS IN LOWER ASSAM

The growth of news media in Bongaigaon district appears to have begun only during the fifties with a total of only 43 journalists joining the media fold upto 1998 excluding the new generation coming up from different remote and rural areas of the district and it all began in Bongaingaon district with Harmohan Chakravorty, born in 1927 at Borshongaon, working as News Editor, AIR, Guwahati in 1981-85, Information Officer, Press Information Bureau, Guwahati, 1971-81, Asstt, Information Officer, PIB, 1965-71, Sub-Editor, Sadiniya Asomiya in 1951-53. It extended to the sixties with Dhanikanta Pathak, born in 1927 at Khamarpara, working as Srijangram Correspondent, Notun Asomiya in 1961 for some years, felicited by Bongaigaon District Journalist Association; Sarmaram Das, born in 1946 at Srijangram, working as correspondent, Nilachal in 1964-71; Gana Batori. Udoy Ch Das, born at Goassaigaon, working as local correspondent, Dainik Asom in 1965-85; Jyotish Barua, born in 1943, died in 1992 at Pachoniya, having worked as Sub-Editor, Dainik Asom, later Staff Reporter, Chief Staff Reporter, Special Correspondent (1965-92) thereof, General Secretary, Assam Journalist Association, Guwahati Press Club, Secretary, Assam Legislative Assembly Journalist Committee; and Amol Kr Das, born in 1944 at Bongaigaon, working as correspondent of Jonombhumi in 1970. During the seventies, Ranjan Kr Chakravorty, born in Bongaigaon, started working as Sub-Editor, The Assam Express, Evening News, and edited Abhijatri and Prakash.. Subhananda Chakravorty, born in 1942 at Deangaon, started woking as Correspondent, Dainik Asom in 1973, Editor, Purba Bharati, 1984.

During the eighties again, Rupnath Mushahary,

born in 1968 at Bijni, started working as Chief Editor, Udangshree in 1990, Editor, Gaudaan in 1994, Chief Editor, Fanjamuthi in 1986, Asstt, Editor, Chan, in 1980-90, Chief Secretary, Bodo Writer's Academy. Ratneswar Basumatary, worked Editor, Jana Batori, Assamese Weekly, Bibungthi, Bodo Weekly, 1995, Notun Nayok, 1992-93, Bishombi, 1987, Neils' Voice, Purbobhash, Assamese-English, 1987, Bidang, Bodo and English in 1982-83. Pranjeet Das, born in 1964 at Bijni, started working as Bijni correspondent, Ajir Asom in 1989, Yug in 1983, Amar Desh. Mousum Mihir Roy, born in 1967 at Abhayapuri, worked as local correspondent, Notun Dainik, Saptahik Istehar, Janakranti, Nagorik, Rashtriya Batori from 1983-89. Ambikacharan Choudhury, born in 1930 at Borpara, started working as Editor, Kamatabani in 1984. Smt Chino Bosumatary, born in 1954 at Bhaulaguri, Chief Editor, Bodcha, Bodo Weekly, 1991, ARNAI, Bodo Fortnightly, 1986, President, Kokrajhar District Journalist Association, Bodoland Journalist Association, All Assam Small Newspapers Association. Koruna Kanti Roy, born in 1960 at Kolbarigaon, Bijni, local correspondent, Dainik Asom in 1988, The Assam Tribune in 1992, Secetary, Bijni Journalist Association, Working President, Bongaigaon District Journalist Association.. Kondorpo Kr Roy, born in 1974 at Kolabari, worked as Manikpur Correspondent, Ajir Asom in 1993, Saptahik Rongpur, Bijni in 1994, Saptahik Borpeeth in 1989-90. Kamal Kanti Chakravorty, born in 1971 at Abahayapuri, started working as Corresondent, Borpeeth in 1990, Ajir Batori, Rongpur, Deubar, The North East Observer, The North East Times, Kajiranga, News Network, as Joint Secretary, Bongaigaon District Journalist Association and Secretary, Abhayapuri Press

Club.

The nineties witnessed growth of journalists like: Heman Pathak, born in 1939 at Abhayapuri, started working as local correspondent, Dainik Asom in 1991, Founder General Secretary, Bongaigaon District Journalist Association, President, Abhayapuri Press Club. Ramananda Kumar, born in 1931 at Peer Howly under Beguchoria district of Bihar, started working as Bongaigaon Corresponent of The Sentinel (Hindi) in 1991 and served as President of Bongaigaon Press Club. Robindra Nath Das, born in 1960 at Bijni, started working as Bongaingaon Correspondent,The North East Times in 1992, President, Bongaigaon Press Club, Bongaigaon District Journalist Association. Badal Krishna Roy, born in 1965 at Bijni, worked as Bongaigaon Corrspondent, Ajir Batori in 1992, received Best Prize in journalism from Ajir Batori in 1992.. Umesh Ch Roy, born in 1968 at North Salmara, local correspondent, Saptahik Deubar in 1993, Saptahik Agrogoti, Secretary, Bongaigaon District Journalist Association.

GOALPARA DISTRICT

So far as Goalpara district is concerned, it all appears to have begun only during the forties and the number of journalists reached a height with 88 journalists joining the media fold in all upto 1998 excluding the new generation coming up from different remote and rural areas of the district and took root beginning with Abdur Rahman Firozi, born near Lakhipur, publisher of Saptahik Biswadoot since 1946. During the fifties, Nripen Barua, born in 1939 and started woring as Goalpara correspondent, Notun Asomiya, Dainik Santidoot, Jonombhumi, Co-Editor, Janakantha, Ratnapeeth (1958-

62), Editor, Saktishel (1954-56), Working President, Goalpara Committee of Celebration of 150 Years of Newspapers in Assam, Felicited by Goalpara District Journalist Association in 1992. Kalyan Singh, born in 1938 at Goalpara, started working as Editor, Janakantha in 1992, Ratnapeeth in 1958-62, Asst Editor, Shaktishel in 1954-56. During the sixties, Gurucharan Das, born in 1936 at Goalpara, started working as Goalpara correspondent, The Assam Tribune in 1963-92. Sarmaram Das, born in 1946 at Srijangram started working as correspondent, Nilachal in 1964-71, Gana Batori. Dr Khiren Roy, born in 1941 at Matia, worked as Editor, The North East Times in 1989-92, Purbachal in 1989-92, Asstt, Editor, Sub-Editor, Correspondent, Special Representative, The Assam Tribune in 1966-89.

It further grew during the seventies with Noresh Das Kalita, born in 1948 started working as Goalpara Correspondent of Dainik Asom in 1979 and served as Secretary, Goalpara District Journalist Association. Gokul Ch Roy, born in 1953 at Bhela Khamar, worked as local correspondent, Purbanchal and Notun Din in 1994, Agradoot, Tinidiniya Batori, Ajir Asom, Rongpur in 1980. M. Ismail Hussain, born in 1950 at Kalyanpur , started working as local correspondent, Saptahik Mujaheed in 1980, Janakantha in 1994.

The eighties witnessed journalists like Mousum Mihir Roy, born in 1967 at Abhayapuri, working as local correspondent, Notun Dainik, Saptahik Istehar, Janakranti, Nagorik, Rashtriya Batori from 1983-89. Sadiniya Prahari in 1985-87, News Star in 1984-85, The Assam Express in 1984, Asst, Editor, Protiti in 1983; Foni Das, born at Sundariya, Barepta in 1943, working as Goalpara

Correspondent, Ajir Asom in 1995, Founder President, Goalpara District Journalist Association 1986-91; Ananata Kr Das, born in 1927 at Dakhinhati, Barepta, working as Dhupdhara Correspondent of Ajir Asom in 1987, Vice-President, Goalpara District Journalist Association; Bhobesh Das, born in 1964 at Lakhipur, woking as local correspondent, Ajir Asom in 1987, Co-Editor, Ratnapeeth Barta in 1991; Naba Kr Mishra, born in 1968 at Dhupdhara, working as Editor, Saptahik Ratnapeeth, Dhupdhara, Asstt Editor, Agradoot in 1988-90, Istehar in 1990-91, Goalpara Correspondent, Dainik Asom; Uttal Kr Das, born in 1960 at Abhayapuri, started working as Correspodnent, Borpeeth in 1988-90. Utpal Chakravorty, born at Uttar Salmara in 1969, working as local correspondent, Saptahik Borpeeth in 1990, Saptahik Istehar, Notun Din, Sandhya Batori, Ajir Asom in 1991, Ajir Batori in 1992, Rongpur in 1994, Organising Secretary, All Assam Journalist Association in 1992, third winner of the year of Best Journalism Award of Ajir Batori for 1994; and Md Dilawar Hussain, born in 1949 at Bordol, started working as local correspondent, The North East Times in 1990.

During the nineties again, Amal Chakravorty, born at Dolgoma, started working as Correspodent, Ajir Songbad, Ratnapeeth, Ajir Batori, Deubar, Agragoti etc, in 1991. Konok Chakravorty, born in 1968 at Chandoria Pathar, Goalpara, started working as Correspondent, Ratnapeeth Barta in 1991, Prakash, Janachetana. Abdul Rashid Ahmed, born in 1973 at Sotisia Khamar, started working as Staff Reporter, Saptahik Mujaheed in 1993. Abu Taleb, born in 1958 at Katlitari, started working as local Correspondent, Dainik Asom, Deubar in 1994. Brojgopal Bhattacharyya, born in 1934 at Goalpara, Editor, Challenger Barta (Karimganj Saptahik) from January 1994. Also, Eusuf Ali, born in 1957 at Karbala , took up pen as freelance journalist and worked as Asstt Secretary, Goalpara District Journalist Association.

KOKRAJHAR DISTRICT

Kokrajhar district appears to have lagged much behind in this respect and the growth of newsmedia seems to have begun too late only during the eighties adding hardly 12 journalists upto 19898 excluding the new generation coming up from different remote and rural areas of the district in the district as a whole with Kalipada Dey, born in 1955 at Bhobanipur Titaguri, started working as local correspondent, Somoy Prabah in 1991, Soptabarta in 1881, Editor, Kokrajhar District Journalist Association in 1993. Bikash Chakravorty, born in 1961 at Titaguri, started working as Senior Sub-Editor and then as I/c Executive Editor, Gana Patrika in 1993-95, Representative, Overland in 1992-93, Sub-Editor, Dainik Yuga Sankha in 1990-92, Kokrajhar Representative, Yuga Sankha in 1985-90, Special Representative, Gana Chabuk in 1982-85. Rajiv Kumar, born in 1970 at Kokrajhar and started working as Dhubri correspondent, Uttarkak in 1989-90 and Sentinel (Hindi) in 1990-91, Sub-Editor, The Sentinel (Hindi) in 1991-93, Asst Editor, Somoy Sutradhar (Hindi Fortnightly) in 1993 and as a Freelancer in 1993.

It grew littler further during the nineties with Abdul Aziz Khan, born in 1963 at Haraputa, working as Gossaigaon Correspondent, The Assam Tribune in 1992 and serving as Vice-President of Kokrajhar District Journalist Association and as Organaising Secretary of Bodoland Journalist Assoication. Jibeswar Koch, born in

1960 at Kolbari, working as Dudhnoi Correspondent of Dainik Asom in 1993; and Gobinda Nath Nath, born at Hadanpara, working as Kokrajhar Correspondent, Dainik Asom in 1995. Also it saw growth in the form of Partho Dev Goswami, born in 1970 at Kokrajhar, working as local correspondent, Ajir Asom; and Satya Narayan Saroswat, born in 1949 at Kokrajhar, working as local correspondent, Purbanchal Prahari.

DHUBRI DISTRICT

The development of news media in Dhubri district appears to have practically begun during the forties and the number of journalists could rise upto a total of 68 only upto 1998 excluding the new generation coming up from different remote and rural areas of the district with Prafulla Kr Chakravorty, born at South Salmara , in 1919, starting to work as local/special correspondent, The Assam Tribune in 1946-92, Jonombhumi in 1952-60, Dainik Asom in 1957-60, The Shillong Times in 1964-65, PTI in 1963-83, The Assam Express in 1972-88, News Star in 1985-89, Eastern Clarion in 1992. Next decade which began in the fifties saw Narayan Ch Sarkar, born in 1935 at Bikrampur, Dhaka, Bangladesh, started working as Asstt, Editor, Lekhakarmi in 1994, Sub-Editor, Gana Patrika in 1994-95, Staff Reporter, Banglabhasha in 1952-53. Joyanta Kr Charkravorty, born in 1930 at Dhubri, started working as local correspondent, Saptahik Abhimat in 1967-80, Ananda Bazar Patarika, Hindustan Standard in 1964-78, Yug Alo in 1952-59. Prithis Narayan Goswami, born in 1940 at Salkocha, started working as the Kokrajhar Correspondent of The Sentinel in 1984, Dainik Asom in 1971-94, Founder Secretary, Kokrajhar District Journalist Association. Animesh Ch Ghosh, worked as Editor,

Mozdoor, published from Dhubri in 1952. Reboti Mohan Dutta Choudhury, born in 1924 at Gauripur, started working as Asstt Editor, The Assam Tribune in 1954, received Sahitya Academy Award in 1994. Bipin Chakravorty, born in Kolkata in 1904, died in 1995, worked as Editor, Freedom Fighter in 1958, Gana Chabuk in 1968, The North East Echo in 1984-95.

During the sixties, Ambunath Sharma, born at Sonakani on March 1, 1943, started working as Golokganj Correspondent, Dainik Asom in 1965. Ambunath Sharma, born at Sonakani in 1943, started working as Golokganj Correspondent, Dainik Asom in 1965. Giasuddin Ahmed, ex-MLA, started working as Editor, Nova Diganta published from Bilashipara in 1967. Sibendra Narayan Mondal, born in 1907 at Koimari, died in May 3, 1989, started working as Published Bi-Lingual Newspaper Prantabashi in 1967. Subhash Chakarvorty, worked as Editor, Goalparar Batori, published form Dhubri,

The decade beginning at the seventies witnessed journalist like: Doyal Paul, born in 1948 in Bangladesh, started working as Bilashipara Correspondent, News Front, Gana Patrika, Assam Express, Notun Asomiya (1972-75). Dinesh Ch Sarkar, born in 1944 at Biskhowa, started working as local correspondent, Gana Chabuk in 1990-91, Saptahik Nilachal in 1974. Amorendra Nath Roy, born in 1941 at Dhubri, started working as local correspondent, The North East Times, Somoy Prabah, Frontier News, Uttar Bonga Songabad (Siliguri) in 1975. Anowar Islam (Advocate), born in 1960 at village Charkasharipara, Hallidayganj of West Garo Hills district, started working as Hatsingimari correspondent, The North East Times, The Assam Tribune, The Telegraph (as freelancer for sometime), Hallidayganj Correspondent, The Shillong Times, The Meghalaya Guardina from 1990-91 onward, also worked as Tura Corresondent, The Assam Tribune for sometime and worked as a Columnist from 1987 onward, starting as a beginner in 1979, received Competition Success Review Commendation Certificate in 1979 for Write up Contest on India of My Dreams, founded Hatsingimari Press Club, served as Founder President thereof starting from 1992-93, pioneered setting up of Mahkuma Press Council, Hatsingimari in 2009, founded and published as Founder Editor, Saptahik Saptadhwani (Bi-Lingual) from Hatsingimari for the first time around 2001,received Rashtriya Rattan Award instituted in memory of Rajiv Gandhi for his "Outstanding Personal Achievments and Distinguished Services to the Nation" in 2004 as a great social activist, followed two time selection for International Gold Star Millenium Award in Bankok (Thailand) first, and then in Nepal, but the same could not be collected by him for private reasons, composed several books and poems besides an far extra-ordinary book on comparative study of religions, namely, Isn't Science A Modern Pharaoh? (Vol.I & II), Vol.I having been released on INTERNET made readily available in E-mail Address: islam_anwar@rediffmail,com.

During the eighties, Gautom Sharma, born at Siliguri under Darjeeling district, West Bengal, worked as Staff Reporter, Abhiruchi in 1995, Special Representative, Rongghor, Bishmoi in 1981-1990, Editing Assistant, Saptahik Asom, Dainik Mahanagar in 1991-92, Executive Editor, Nilachal in 1993-95, Story Writer, Patliputra Times, Patna and Noyaduniya, Bhopal, Press Photographer.

Imdad Ahmed, born in 1939 at Kakripara village , worked as Asst Editor, Nilachal, Editing Assistant, Weekly Express, News Star during 1982-86. Momtazuddin Ahmed, started working as Editor, Insani Awaz published from Bilashipara in 1982. Ardhendu Nath Chakravorty, born in 1946 at Hakama, started working as local correspondent, Purab in 1994, The Assam Tribune in 1992, The North East Times in 1991, Purbachal in 1991-92, The North East Echo in 1983-85, Gana Chabuk in 1983-85. Prodip Kr, Dey, born in 1961 at Sapotgram, started working as local correspondent og Gana Chabuk in 1983. Bikash Sarkar, born in 1965 at Goyerkata, Jalpaiguri under West Bengal, started working as Cartoonist, Somoy Prabah in 1990, Janapath Samachar in 1988-90, Sahitya Editor, Bichitra Biswa in 1985-88. Samsuddin Ahmed, born in 1948 at Airmary, started working as South Salamara Correspondent, Dainik Asom in 1986, served as Founder President, South Salmara Sub-Divisional Journalist Association. Sushil Kr Jain, born in 1960 at Dhubri, started working as local correspondent, Uttarkal in 1994, Gana Chabuk in1993, Biswaroopa in 1986. Deepak Kr, Medhi, Born in 1963 at Mowatari, Chapar, started working as local Correspondent, Ajir Asom in 1988, Founder Secretary, Chapar Press Club. Pranab Acharya, born in 1952 at Golokganj, started as Sub-Editor, Giyandweep in 1987-89. Sadiniya Nagorik in 1988, General Secretary, Bodoland Journalist Association, Secretary, Bongaigaon Press Club, Organising Secretary, All Assam Journalist Association. Druba Kr Gupta, born in 1967 at Dhubri, started working as local Correspondent, Uttarkal, Sentinel (Hindi) in 1988. Deepak Kr Medhi, born in 1963 at Mowatari, Chapar, started working as local

Correspondent, Ajir Asom in 1988, Founder Secretary, Chapar Press Club. Pijush Kanti Saha, born on June 29, 1965 at Bilashipara, started working as Sub-Editor, Somoy Prabah in 1989, Somokal in 1988-89.

During the nineties again, Atma Ram Agarwala (Advocate), Mankachar worked as local correspondent of Purbanchal Prahari (Hindi Daily) in 1990. Bijoy Kr Sharma, born in 1964 at Dhubri, started working as Representative, The North East Times in 1993, local correspondent, The North East Observer in 1992-93, The Assam Express in 1990-91, Staff Reporter, The North East Times in 1991-92. Pinaki Chakravorty, born in 1968 at College Nagar, Dhubri, started working as local correspondent, Notun Dainik in 1990. Hiranya Kumar Nath, born in 1954 at Gobordhan, started working as Bilashipara Correspondent, Ajir Batori in 1991, Notun Dainik in 1990, Ajir Asom in 1990, Rongpur in 1994. Altaf Hussain Ahmed, born in 1973 at Bilashipara started working as Representative, Mouchak in 1991 etc. Kameshwar Mishra, born in 1939 in Bihar, started working as Bilashipara Correspondent, Purbanchal Prahari in 1991, The Hindi Sentinel. Tarkeshwar Paul, born in 1965 at Dhubri, started working as local correspondent, Somoy Prabah in 1992, Gana Patrika (Four Month), Independent News Agency (Six Month), Overland (Calcutta-1 year). Johirul Islam, born in 1965 at Fulerchar, started working as Hatsingimari correspondent of Dainik Asom from 1992, served as founder Secretary of Hatsingimari Press Club, worked as founder Asst Editor, Bi-lingual Saptahik Saptadhwani, Hatsingimari, received District Best Youth Award from Nehru Yuva Mancha, Dhubri Branch in 1995. Binoy Bhushan Sen, started working as Staff Reporter,

Dainik Yugoshankha in 1995, Special Representative, Uttar Bonga Songbad, published from Siliguri in 1992, Former Sports Correspondent, Sports World, published from Kolkata, Founder Editor, Sorbolok (Bi-lingual Weekly, Bengali and English), Founder, Awaj and X-Ray, Former Representative, Trilotta and Pratyahik Samachar. Imdadul Islam Mondal (Moni), born in 1960 at village Gotabari, Hazirhat (Hatsingimari), started working as local correspondent, Notun Dainik from 1994, Saptahik Purbachal form 1993, Saptahik Sadin from 1993, Ajir Asom from 1993, Abhimot, 2004, Saptahik Saptadhwani, 2001, Adinor Sombad, 2007, secured first position in article competition organized under the aegis of Hidayat(Hikmot) on "Musalman Hokolor Dur Abosthar Prashanga". Dipak Ghosh, born in 1966 at Coochbehar, West Bengal, started working as Sub-Editor, Somoy Prabah in 1994, Gana Patrika in 1993-94. Abdul Jalil Sheikh, born in 1968 at Modhusolmari, started working as local correspondent, Gana Chabuk in 1994. Joydeep Barua, Dhubri Correspondent, Asomiya Pratidin in 1995. Arun Mahanta, born in 1965 at Baniyapara, started working as Staff Reporter, Bodoland Khourang in 1995. Abdul Akher Amin (Bokul), born in 1968 at Fulerchar, started working as Correspondent, Natun Dainik, Saptahik Dapon in 1996, worked as a local correspondent of the Bi-lingual Shaptahik Saptadhwani, Hatsingimari in 2001, Dhubri Staff Reporter, Dainik Batori Kakot in 2009, founder President, Mahkuma Press Council, Hatsingimari, also publisher and editor, Zinjiram 2nd edition and Prtonidhi 1st edition, published as "Mukhopatra" of Asom Shaitya Sabha, Hatsingimari Branch, Editor, Smriti Grantha "Abhimot" in 2008, also published an article on the life of former Minister of Assam, Jehirul Islam in 2009 in Dainik Batori Kakot, received "Smarok Bota" given away in memory of late M A Sattar, reputed journalist of Tezpur in 2009.

Of the older generation of the journalists, Dilip Kr Chakravorty, born in 1952 at Dhubri, started working as Editor, Gana Chabuk and General Secretary, Dhubri District Journalist Association, Vice-President, All Assam Small Newspapers Association, and as Secretary of Dhubri District Committee of Celebration of 150 Years of Newspapers in Assam. Sultan Amin, born in 1959 at Mankachar, worked for sometime as local correspondent of Gana Chabuk of Dhubri. Forhad Ali Ahmed, born at Kakripara, Mankachar, started working as local Correspondent, Asomiya Khobor, Amar Asom, Asomiya Pratidin, Dainik Agradoot, presently working actively as TV Correspondent, NEWS LIVE, serving as Vice-President, Mahkuma Press Council, Hatsingimari. Akramuzzaman, born at Gajarikandi, Kukurmara (Mankachar), started working as local Correspondent, Dainik Agradoot, Asstt. Editor, Saptahik Saptadhwani, Hatsingimari in 2001. Robindra Nath Choudhury, born at Dhubri, started working as Editor, Simanta Prohari. Subhash Ch Paul, born in 1927 at Dhubri, started working as Editor, Abhimot (Bi-Lingual). Dipankar Roy, born in 1956 at Alipurduar under West Bengal, started working as Editor, Eastern Clarion, Correspondent, Amrit Bazar Patrika, The North East Times. Mohesh Ch Roy, born in 1947 at Dakhin Tukresrchora, started working as local Correspondent, Gana Chabuk, Prantabashi. Khalilur Rahman, born at Dhubri, started working as Editor, Pohor (Saptahik).

Of the present generation journalists, Monowar Hussain, born in 1975 at Kanaimara, Hatsingimari, started working as Mankachar Correspondent, Aji in 2007, Staff Reporter, Dainik Batori Kakot, worked for Asomiya Protidin for sometime, published articles etc. in Gana Chabuk, Smriti Grantha, Papori etc., serving as Secretary, Mahkuma Press Council, Hatsingimari Monowar Hussain Ahmed, born at village Fekamari, Hatsingimari, started working as local Correspondent, Janasadharan, serving as Publicity Secretary, Mahkuma Press Council, Hatsingimari. Nashiruddin Ahmed, born at Charkasharipara village, Hatsingiamri, started working as local correspondent, The Sentinel. Mohibul Islam, Kharuabanda, Hatsingimari, started working as local correspondent & as Asst Secretary, Mahkuma Press Council, Hatsingimari. Mafizur Rahman, Hatsingimari, started working as local correspondent & as Organizing Secretary, Mahkuma Press Council, Hatsingimari. Abu Bokkar Siddique, Hatsingimari, started working as local correspondent & as Asst Secretary, Mahkuma Press Council, Hatsingimari.

NALBARI DISTRICT

The news media in Nalbari district appears to have started growing fast in the pre-Independence period itself and reached a height surpassing a total of more than 142 journalists upto 1998 excluding the new generation coming up from different remote and rural areas of the district, and might have created a history of its own beginning with the emergence of prominent pre-Independence period journalists like Satish Ch Kakati, born in 1914 at Ulubari under Nalbari district is especially noteworthy, who dedicated life to the service of the nation during the thirties and forties. Mr. Kakati had started working as

Guwahati Representative of Hindustan Standard, Ananda Bazar Patrika and Associate Press of India during 1937-47. He also worked as Asst Editor, The Assam Tribune during 1951-63, Editor, Asom Bani (1955-80), Editor, The Assam Tribune (1963-76) and served as Vice-President, All India Newspapers Editor's Conference during 1975-77, as President during 1955-85, Founder President, All Assam Journalist Association during 1956-72. and was a regular Columnist of The Statesman, The Assam Tribune, Indian Express, The Telegraph etc., received Padmashree Award and Tamrapatra (as Freedom Fighter) and was a Sahitya Pensioner. Secondly, Pratap Talukdar, born in 1902, died in 1966 at Ulabori, worked as Publisher and Editor, Amar Gaon (Fortnightly) in 1943, Kamrup (Weekly) in 1949. Thirdly, Dr Promod Ch Bhattacharyya, born in 1925 at Digheligaon, started working as Sub-Editor, Dainik Asomiya in 1947-49, Notun Asomiya in 1950-51, Asst, Editor, Rongghar (Child Magazine), Ramdheunu, President, Kamrup District Sahitya Conference, Tamupurm Shahitya Pensioner.

During the fifties and sixties, Dr. Durgeswar Sharma, born at Borsimliya (Bukiya) in 1931, started working as Asst Editor, Santidoot in 1953-58, Pragjyoti in 1960-63, North Guwahati Correspondent, Nilachal in 1962-63, The Assam Tribune in 1958-60, Notun Asomiya in 1962-65, Sahityik Pensioner. Riju Hazarika, born at Hazrapara in 1940, started working as Proof Reader, The Assam Tribune in 1960-62, Chief Editor, Boloy in 1983, Koma in 1982, Editor, Asomy in 1958-59, Asstt, Editor, Pancharatna in 1959. Gaurikanta Talukdar, born in 1885, died in 1966 at Chamata, started working as Editor, Deedpak (Monthly) in 1954-66.

During late sixties, early seventies, eighties and nineties to some extent, Bhupendra Nath Sharma, born at Amoyapur in 1935, died in 1983, worked as Sub-Editor, The Assam Tribune in 1960-62. Labnya Molla Barua, born in 1929 at Nijopkuwa, started working as Proof Reader, Notun Asomiya, and then as Sub-Editor (1962-65). Biraj Das, born in 1940 at Komarkuchi, started working as Staff Reporter, The Assam Tribune in 1963-66. Hori Barman, born in 1944 at Teresia, worked as local correspondent, Tinidiniya Baori, Rashtriya Batori, 1983-84, Ganatantra, 1963-66, Ratnapeeth, 1965-66, Notun Asomiya, 1963. Dharam Ch Jain, born in 1944, started working as local correspondent, Purbanchal Prahori in 1989-90, The Sentinel in 1983-90, News Star, Purbojyoti in 1964-75. Bodon Lahkar, born at Lahkarpara, Baharghat in 1942, worked as Editor, Sadiniya Songabad, published from Tezpur in 1989, Executive Editor, Mohajati in 1965. Jiten Sharma, born at West Chamata in 1938. started working as Producer of Mobile Theatre of Assam, local correspondent, Dainik Asom in 1965-90. Chandra Bhusan Sharma, born at Bormurikona in 1943, started working as Editor, Simanta Dhwani, Asstt Editor, Alok in 1967-72. Aboni Kumar Bhattacharyya, born in 1949 at Mohkholi, started working as Sr. Journalist, United News of India, Itanagar in 1982, earlier served in different post under United News of India from 1968 onward. Hemchandra Barma Mozumdar, born in 1901 at Namdonga, worked as local correspondent, Dainik Jonombhumi, Asom Batori, Notun Asomiya, President, North Kamrup Journalist Association, 1968-73, Freedom Fighter, Honoured with Tamrapatra. Satish Ch Sharma, born at Adatrari in 1947, started working as UNI Bureau Chief in 1980, Manager,

Guwalior Branch of UNI in 1975-80, Shillong Representative, UNI in 1969-75,President, Journalist Union of Assam in 1992,Guwahati Press Club in 1992-95. Dr Bhagiroth Kalita, born in 1947 at Sadndhya, started working as Proof Reader, The Assam Tribune in 1969 and then Sub-Editor, then Chief Sub-Editor and then Asstt, Editor upto 1990 and finally Deputy Editor, The Assam Tribune by 1991. Saleuddin Choudhury, born in 1948 at Banpatkuchi, started working as Executive Editor, Nagorik in 1992, Founder Editor, Asom Songbad in 1991, Asst Editor, Agradoot in 1975-91, Editing Assistant, Asom Raiz in 1970-75. Prankrishna Das, born in 1942 at Tihu, started working as Tihu Correspondent, The Assam Tribune in 1981, Agradoot in 1976, Dainik Jonombhumi in 1970-72, Founder President, Tihu Press Club in 1988, Jt Editor, Uttar Kamrup Journalist Association in 1977-81, Working President, Celebration Committee of Nalbari district of 150 Years of Newspapers in Assam.

During the late seventies, eighties and nineties again, Konoksen Deka, born in 1933 at Belsor, started working as Editor, Agradoot in 1971, received Rashtriya Nagorik Award in 1993 and Jnenor Sagor Award in 1994. Atun Sharma, born at Piplibari in 1953, started working as Representative UNI in 1983, Chief Sub-Editor, Assam Express in 1977-83. Tapan Das, born in 1957 at Nalbari, started working as Chitra correspondent, Notun Dainik in 1987, Awakash in 1982-86, Piyom in 1982-83, Silpir Prithvi in 1979, received Nobin Surya Award in 1991. Dilip Sharma, born at Balikuchi in 1958 started working as Editor, Budhbar in 1995, Abhiruchi in 1979. Bolendra Mohan Chakravorty, born at Bormurikon, Borbari worked as Publisher & Editor, Abhiruchi in 1979,1980, Founder

President, Assam Sports Journalist Association and Treasurer, Indian Sports Journalist Association..

Similarly, of the other prominent journalists of the eighties and nineties are: Kamal Kr Jain, born in 1965 at Nalbari started working as Representative, Jagriti in 1983, local correspondent, Protidin and Tinidiniya Batori in 1982, Edited Bikiron. Sailendra Narayan Goswami, born in 1954 at Naptipara, started working as local correspondent of Amar Khobor, Asstt Editor, Amar Progoti in 1984, Abhiruchi in 1984. Noren Das, born in 1955, died in 1969 at Atghoriya, started working as Editor, Amar Sahitya in 1988-94, Member of Editorial Board, Saptahik Janajeevan in 1986-94. Babul Barua, born in 1943 at Komarkuchi, worked as Chief of Bureau, PTI, Silchar from June 1986 onward. Rohini Medhi, born in 1956 at Sialmari, started working as Barama Correspondent, The Sentinel in 1989, Nalbari Sadar Representative, Ajir Asom in 1990, Tihu Representative, Ajir Batori in 1993-97, Founder Secetary, Baska Press Club in 1989, President in 1995-97, Secretary, Nalbari District Journalist Association in 1992-93, 94-97, Secretary, Nalbari District Committee of Celebration of 150 Years of Newspapers in Assam. Ramani Barman, born in 1956 at Solmari, worked as Correspondent, Notun Dainik in 1990 onward, later Special Corresponent from 1995, President, West Nalbari Press Club, Secretary, Nalbari Press Council, Asstt, Secretary, Nalbari District Journalist Associaion, received Best Journalist Award in 1994 and 1995 occupying third and first position respectively.

Profiles of majority journalists of the eighties and nineties having already been presented above, it may not be wise to add here that Yadovsen Deka, born in 1940 at

Belsor, started working as local correspondent, Ajir Asom in 1991, Editor, Moharothi, Novaurmi. Rajdhar Deka, born in 1952 at Mukalmua, started working as Azara Correspondent of Ajir Asom in 1991, The North East Observer in 1992, Saptahik Rongpur in 1992. Lila Devi, born in 1968 at Botisor, joined as Sub-Editor, Puwali and Purbachal in 1992. Narayan Goswami, born in 1956 at Koithalkuchi, started working as Howly Correspondent of Ajir Batori in 1992 and served as Secretary, Howly Press Club. Ganapoti Chourang Bodo, born in 1970 at Kolabari Barama, started working as local correspondent, Bodocha (Bodo Saptahik) in 1993. Khogen Bhuyan, born in 1958 at Simlabari (Na Bosti),started working as Baganpara Correspondent, Ajir Batori in 1994,Secretary, Baska Press Club,1995-97.

Likewise, Jibon Dauka, born in 1963 at Koriya, started working as freelance Press Photographer, Chitra Songbad, Notun Dainik in 1983, Puwali, Bismoi, Prantik in 1990, Akani, Deubar(Saptahik) in 1992-95. Anil Kr Deka, born at Beelpar, started working as Chief Editor, Anupam in 1985, received first prize in the National-cum-International Convention of Editors Exihibition in 1987 organized under the aegis of Indian Small and Medium Newspapers Federation. Haladhar Haloi, born at Haribhanga in 1963. started working as local correspondent of Saptahik Janajeevan in 1987-92, then Sub-Editor thereof in 1992-93. Somesh Deka, born in 1961 at Bongaon, started working as Special Repesentative (Sibsagar), Nilachal, News Star in 1995, Saptahik Janombhumi in 1993-94, Amar Khobor in 1994, Kolom in 1987-90, New East News Line in 1987, Abhiruchi in 1987, Sports Correspondent, Dainik Asom in 1994, Staff

Repporter, Notun Din in 1990-94. Bhupen Barman, born in 1960 at Nodola, worked as Staff Reporter/Publisher, Saptahik Janajeevan, 1988. Arup Kr Sharma, born at Digholi on August 15, 1967 started working as Representative, Saptahik Janambhumi in 1994, Asom Bani in 1988-89, Dainik Janambhumi in 1988-89, Executive Editor, Pylon in 1994, Sub-Editor, Rajdhani Batori in 1990, Saptahik Asom in 1990, Sub-Editor, News Front, then Executive Editor, Amorjyoti, Editor, Saptahik Agrogoti in 1992. Prodipjyoti Kumar, born in 1966 at Neejbahjani, started working as Asstt, Editor, Saptahik Asom in 1989-92 and worked as Correspondent of Mahanagar. Upen Deka, born in 1971 at Musalpur, started working as local correspondent, Purbachal in 1992, Ajir Songbad in 1993-94, Amorjyoti in 1991-92,Agrogoti in 1991-92, Istehar in 1989-90, Asomiya Pratidin in 1995. Romen Kalita, born in 1972 at Ulubari, started working as Borbhog Correspondent, Bataboron in 1989, Purbachal in 1992-94, Dainik Asom and The Assam Tribune in 1994. Jyotish,Bhattacharyya, born at Nij Chamata, started working as local correspondent, Notun Dainik in 1989-92, Ajir Asom, Ajir Songbadin 1994, received Best Sports Journalism Award of Ajir Songbad newspaper for 1994. Utpal Mena, born at Belsor, started working as Sub-Editor, Ajir Songbad in 1994, Editor, Moharothi in 1989-90. Kamal Kr. Bhagwati, born in 1968 at Koithalkuchi, started working as Asstt, Editor and Special Representatiave, Chitra Songbad in 1992 and 1990-92 respectively, Joint Secretary, All Assam Chitra Journalist Assoication in 1993. Birendra Nath Barman, born at Nalbari, worked as local correspondent, Ajir Batori, 1990, Special Correspondent Award,1994 given away by Ajir Batori.

And yet, Jiten Sharma, born at Nalbari, started working as local correspondent, Ajir Asom in 1991, Staff Reporter, Amar Nalbari. Lakhimi Roy Medhi, born at Borkuriha in 1969, started working as Sub-Editor, Saptahik Nagorik in 1992, Asom Songbad in 1991. Ajit Sharma, born at Dakhingaon in 1963, started working as local correspondent, Ajir Batori in 1991-94, later Staff Reporter, received 2nd Best Prize of Ajir Batori in 1992. Bolendra Narayan Choudhury, born in 1960 at Helecha, started working as correspondent, Hajor Batori in 1991. Kumud Ch Deka, born in 1961 at Bortola, started working as Proof Reader, Agradoot in 1991. Bipul Bhattacharyya, born at Helecha, started working as local correspondent, Saptah Darpan in 1992. Dr Amarendra Kalita, born at Chandkuchi, started working as Tihu Correspodent, The Eastern Clarion in 1992 and was awarded by The Eastern Clarion for significant contribution to journalism. Ponkoj Bezbaruah, born in 1972 at Nannatari, worked Tihu Correspondent, Rongpur, 1993, Editor, Bagh (Magazine) in 1993. Promod Barman, born in November, 1962 at Arora, worked as Halflong Correspondent, Asom Songbad, 1993, Editor, The Peoples, 1995.

Also, Guneswar Koiborto, born in 1966 at Goldigholi started working as Mukalmua Correspondent of Dainik Asom, Ajir Songbad, Agradoot, received Award on Mufissil Journalism in 1993. Monoranjan Talukdar, born in 1967 at Bohjani, started working as Sports Correspondent, Ajir Songbad in 1994. Dhrubajyoti Sharma, born in 1971, started working as Nalbari Special Correspondent, Rongpur in 1994. Anil Kr Mozumdar, born in 1971 at Ghagrapar started working as Ghagrapar Correspondent, Asomiya Protidin in 1995, Editor, Mizink in 1994, Founder Secretary Pub-Nalbari Pess Guild. Upen Kalita, born in 1971, started working as Proof Reader, Ajir Songbad and Jonokranti in 1994. Promod Kalita, born in 1968 at Balitora, started working as Sub-Editor, Ajir Songbad in 1994. Deepak Kalita, born in 1972 at Boragra, started working as Staff Reporter of Nagorik in 1994. Giasuddin Ahmed, born at Borigaon worked as Chief Editor, Projonma in 1994.

To add a little more data, Kaliram Barman, born in 1885, died in 1971 at Mohjepara, Chamata worked as Editor, Biswabarta, Assamese Version of a Govt.Bengali Newspaper published from Dhaka. Dr. Nogen Choudhury, born in 1949, started working as Editor, Rup-Rekha, Asst, Editor, Amar Abhijan, Editing Assistant, Agradoot. Alokesh Thakuria, born in 1969 at Gormara (Barama) started working as correspondent, Saptah Darpon from Barama. Dulal Ch Bhuyan, born in 1915, died in 1977 at Khudra Kulhati, started working as Founder Editor, Saptahik Janambhumi Jogendra Narayan Choudhury, born in 1919 at Khatabari, started working as Sub-Editor, later Chief Sub-Editor, The Assam Tribune, Corespondent, Hindustan Standard. Fonindra Kalita, born in 1932 at Arora, started working as Asstt Editor and Correspondent of Jona Batori, Asom Sangbad, Rongpur, Asom Bani, Santidoot, Asom Batori, Jana Siksha, Sadiniya Asomiya, Notun Asomiya, Ajir Batori, Dainik Asom Dinesh Goswami, born in 1936 at Nalbari, served as Desk Assistant in Amar Pragati, Asom Rize, Agradoot, Nagorik, The North East Times.. Mukul Kr. Sharma, born at Nijpokua on January 9, 1956 started working as Editor, Jagrota Prohori, Pohar.

Before I conclude, it may not be out of place to

mention here that owing to space problems, most of the data of many more prominent journalists working in different districts and subdivisions in Lower Assam Division could not be included in this article. Nevertheless, I will perhaps fail in my duty to do justice to myself unless I put a line to boastfully claim today herein itself and say that journalism, more precisely the moffisil journalism has undoubtedly reached by now almost every nook and corner even in the remotest rural areas in all the districts of the State, and the number of journalists has far surpassed the general expectation in Lower Assam Division by 2010, with no less efforts made at different stages of both pre-Independence and post-Independence to go for founding and publishing newspapers on larger, smaller and medium scales almost in every growing district and subdivisional townships in the State, in which the Lower Assam Division has not at all lagged behind under any scale.

The news media which includes television channels and female journalists as well both at the government and private levels also has fast developed with the advent of 21st century and the number of TV Correspondents/Photographers including female journalists having shown a fast-rising trend giving coverages to the remotest villages, while the growth of Press Clubs or Press Councils including Journalaists Assoications in every district and subdivisional headquarters has registered an all time high record in Lower Assam Division, although the number in other Divisions also may not be less than that of Lower Assam Division under the given rate.

www.ingramcontent.com/pod-product-compliance
Lightning Source LLC
LaVergne TN
LVHW050428160726
843469LV00041B/1271

* 9 7 8 9 3 5 4 5 8 0 5 1 2 *